White Buildings

Hart Crane

白屋

哈特・柯瑞恩 著　林熙強 譯

目次

14 LEGEND

18 BLACK TAMBOURINE

20 EMBLEMS OF CONDUCT

22 MY GRANDMOTHER'S LOVE LETTERS

26 SUNDAY MORNING APPLES
    To William Sommer

30 PRAISE FOR AN URN
    In Memoriam: Ernest Nelson

34 GARDEN ABSTRACT

15 傳說

19 黑色鈴鼓

21 道行的象徵

23 姥姥的情書

27 星期天早晨的蘋果
    致威廉・索默

31 甕之頌
    紀念厄尼斯特・尼爾森

35 果園抽象畫

36　TARK MAJOR

40　CHAPLINESQUE

44　PASTORALE

48　IN SHADOW

52　THE FERNERY

54　NORTH LABRADOR

56　REPOSE OF RIVERS

60　PARAPHRASE

37　死板的大調

41　卓別林調調

45　田園曲

49　在暗影中

53　蕨圃

55　北拉布拉多

57　河的長眠

61　另一種說法

64	POSSESSIONS
68	LACHRYMAE CHRISTI
74	PASSAGE
80	THE WINE MENAGERIE
88	RECITATIVE
92	FOR THE MARRIAGE OF FAUSTUS AND HELEN
112	AT MELVILLE'S TOMB
116	VOYAGES

65　擁有

69　基督之淚

75　時光通道

81　醇酒動物園

89　宣敘調

93　為浮士德與海倫成婚而作

113　在梅爾維爾墓前

117　遠航

140　注釋

145　譯後記

White Buildings

LEGEND

As silent as a mirror is believed
Realities plunge in silence by . . .

I am not ready for repentance;
Nor to match regrets. For the moth
Bends no more than the still
Imploring flame. And tremorous
In the white falling flakes
Kisses are,—
The only worth all granting.

It is to be learned—
This cleaving and this burning,
But only by the one who
Spends out himself again.

Twice and twice
(Again the smoking souvenir,
Bleeding eidolon!) and yet again.

傳說

一如明鏡無聲，所映無疑
現實也深陷靜默……

我還未做好懺悔的準備；
實亦無事可悔。因為飛蛾
的撲身只向著依然
乞求的烈焰。而在
片片飄落的雪朵中顫動著
唯獨只有吻，——
值得所有的付出。

得以體會——
如此粉身碎骨，如此烈焰灼身，
只有那個
願意再次窮盡自己的人。

再一次，再一次，
（灼身的焦煙是紀念，
也是淌著血的幻象！）然後一次又一次。

Until the bright logic is won
Unwhispering as a mirror
Is believed.

Then, drop by caustic drop, a perfect cry
Shall string some constant harmony,—
Relentless caper for all those who step
The legend of their youth into the noon.

直到這麼做的理由得以
似明鏡悄無聲息
所映卻信而無疑。

然後是一滴一滴腐蝕的淚,一聲完美的哭喊
串成一種永不停歇的和聲,——
那是無休無止的歡騰,只為那風華正茂
上演著青春傳奇的人們。

BLACK TAMBOURINE

The interests of a black man in a cellar
Mark tardy judgment on the world's closed door.
Gnats toss in the shadow of a bottle,
And a roach spans a crevice in the floor.

Æsop, driven to pondering, found
Heaven with the tortoise and the hare;
Fox brush and sow ear top his grave
And mingling incantations on the air.

The black man, forlorn in the cellar,
Wanders in some mid-kingdom, dark, that lies,
Between his tambourine, stuck on the wall,
And, in Africa, a carcass quick with flies.

黑色鈴鼓

地窖裡黑人感興趣的事
在世界緊閉的大門上標示了姍姍來遲的判決。
蚊蚋在酒瓶的影子裡衝撞,
一隻蟑螂跨越地板的縫隙。

伊索,不得不沉思默想,
隨龜兔一起找到天堂;
他的墳頭上蓋著狐尾和豬耳
空氣裡混合著咒語。

黑人,在地窖裡孤苦伶仃,
遊蕩於某個中間的國度,黑暗,位於,
釘在牆上,他的鈴鼓,
和,非洲,蒼蠅旋繞的一具腐屍之間。

EMBLEMS OF CONDUCT

By a peninsula the wanderer sat and sketched
The uneven valley graves. While the apostle gave
Alms to the meek the volcano burst
With sulphur and aureate rocks . . .
For joy rides in stupendous coverings
Luring the living into spiritual gates.

Orators follow the universe
And radio the complete laws to the people.
The apostle conveys thought through discipline.
Bowls and cups fill historians with adorations,—
Dull lips commemorating spiritual gates.

The wanderer later chose this spot of rest
Where marble clouds support the sea
And where was finally borne a chosen hero.
By that time summer and smoke were past.
Dolphins still played, arching the horizons,
But only to build memories of spiritual gates.

道行的象徵 [1]

半島上流浪者兀坐勾畫
崎嶇山谷間的墓壘。當使徒施捨
謙卑者的那一刻，火山迸發
出硫磺和金色岩石⋯⋯
因為喜樂藉令人驚嘆的掩護承載，
誘惑生者進入屬靈的門道。

雄辯家遵循宇宙之道
向世人廣播整套律法。
使徒透過戒律傳達思想。
杯盤中的崇拜餵飽歷史學家，——
遲鈍的嘴唇紀念著屬靈的門道。

流浪者後來選擇了這片駐足之地，
那裡珠雲擎托大海
終於誕生一位神選的英雄。
那時夏天和煙霧已經過去。
海豚依然遊戲，弧起地平線，
但只是為了緬懷屬靈的門道。

MY GRANDMOTHER'S LOVE LETTERS

There are no stars tonight
But those of memory.
Yet how much room for memory there is
In the loose girdle of soft rain.

There is even room enough
For the letters of my mother's mother,
Elizabeth,
That have been pressed so long
Into a corner of the roof
That they are brown and soft,
And liable to melt as snow.

Over the greatness of such space
Steps must be gentle.
It is all hung by an invisible white hair.
It trembles as birch limbs webbing the air.

And I ask myself:

姥姥的情書

今晚沒有星星
只有記憶裡的星星。
柔雨如漸寬的衣帶環繞周身
而記憶的空間究竟多麼寬廣。

原來甚至寬廣到
放得下我媽媽的媽媽伊莉莎白
的老情書,
那些長年塞在
天花板一角的老情書
現在已經斑黃菸萎,
一不小心就會像雪片飄融。

足蹈如此浩瀚的空間,
一步一步都得輕盈。
像是給一根看不見的白頭髮拎著。
顫顫巍巍就像樺樹枝在編織空氣。

於是我問自己:

"Are your fingers long enough to play
Old keys that are but echoes:
Is the silence strong enough
To carry back the music to its source
And back to you again
As though to her?"

Yet I would lead my grandmother by the hand
Through much of what she would not understand;
And so I stumble. And the rain continues on the roof
With such a sound of gently pitying laughter.

「手指是否修長到足以彈奏
只響回音的老琴鍵:
這靜默是否強大到
足以把樂聲傳回源頭
也再次傳回給你
一如傳回給她?」

而我想要牽起我姥姥的手
帶她穿越她無法理解的形形色色;
我因此絆了一跤。而雨繼續落在屋頂
那聲音就像一陣輕柔憐憫的笑。

SUNDAY MORNING APPLES

To William Sommer

The leaves will fall again sometime and fill
The fleece of nature with those purposes
That are your rich and faithful strength of line.

But now there are challenges to spring
In that ripe nude with head
                           reared
Into a realm of swords, her purple shadow
Bursting on the winter of the world
From whiteness that cries defiance to the snow.

A boy runs with a dog before the sun, straddling
Spontaneities that form their independent orbits,
Their own perennials of light
In the valley where you live
                        (called Brandywine).

星期天早晨的蘋果

致威廉・索默 [2]

改天樹葉還會再次飄落
藉你筆觸下豐富又忠實的力量
鋪滿大自然的羊毛。

不過眼下的挑戰正衝著春天而來:
那成熟的裸女把頭
     伸進了
劍的國度,而她紫色的影子
從對白雪嗤之以鼻的白裡
倏然出現在這個世界的冬天。

男孩帶著狗跑在太陽前面,跨越
自然而然之下他們各自形成的軌道,
他們各懷長年不衰的光
在你居住的山谷
    (名為白蘭地酒)。

I have seen the apples there that toss you secrets,—
Beloved apples of seasonable madness
That feed your inquiries with aerial wine.
Put them again beside a pitcher with a knife.
And poise them full and ready for explosion—
The apples, Bill, the apples!

SUNDAY MORNING APPLES *To William Sommer*

我在那裡見過蘋果向你吐露祕密，——
可愛的蘋果帶著應時的瘋狂
用虛無飄渺的酒滿足你的探求。
再一次把蘋果擱在壺邊，放上把刀。
穩穩擺好靜態準備靈感的爆發——
蘋果，老哥，那些蘋果啊！

PRAISE FOR AN URN

In Memoriam: Ernest Nelson

It was a kind and northern face
That mingled in such exile guise
The everlasting eyes of Pierrot
And, of Gargantua, the laughter.

His thoughts, delivered to me
From the white coverlet and pillow,
I see now, were inheritances—
Delicate riders of the storm.

The slant moon on the slanting hill
Once moved us toward presentiments
Of what the dead keep, living still,
And such assessments of the soul

As, perched in the crematory lobby,

甕之頌

紀念厄尼斯特・尼爾森[3]

那是一張和藹的北方人臉孔
這樣流亡者的外表下混合著
啞劇丑角[4]永久的眼神
還有巨人國王[5]的朗笑。

從素白的衾與枕
他的想法,傳遞給我,
我現在明白,是一種傳承——
飆風中纖弱的騎士。

斜斜的丘上吊著斜斜的月
一度教我們隱隱感覺
那逝者原來保有的,仍然活著,
也讓我們如此估定靈魂。

暫棲火葬場的大廳,

The insistent clock commented on,
Touching as well upon our praise
Of glories proper to the time.

Still, having in mind gold hair,
I cannot see that broken brow
And miss the dry sound of bees
Stretching across a lucid space.

Scatter these well-meant idioms
Into the smoky spring that fills
The suburbs, where they will be lost.
They are no trophies of the sun.

時鐘的滴答未嘗止息,
那聲響也觸及
我們應時的光榮讚美。

然而心中所記仍是一頭金髮,
眼中所見自不是你破碎面容,
我懷念蜜蜂單調的嗡鳴
在清澈的空間蔓延開來。

就把這些善意的詞語
撒向瀰漫在城郊煙濛濛的春天,
詞語也終將在此消散。
那不是在豔陽底下唾手可得的東西。

GARDEN ABSTRACT

The apple on its bough is her desire,—
Shining suspension, mimic of the sun.
The bough has caught her breath up, and her voice,
Dumbly articulate in the slant and rise
Of branch on branch above her, blurs her eyes.
She is prisoner of the tree and its green fingers.

And so she comes to dream herself the tree,
The wind possessing her, weaving her young veins,
Holding her to the sky and its quick blue,
Drowning the fever of her hands in sunlight.
She has no memory, nor fear, nor hope
Beyond the grass and shadows at her feet.

果園抽象畫

樹枝上的蘋果是她的渴望，——
懸掛半空閃耀，太陽的擬態。
樹枝跟隨她的呼吸，她的聲音，
在頂上枝枝杈杈的起起伏伏之間
默不作聲卻暢所欲言，朦朧了她的雙眼。
綠色的手指已讓她成為樹的囚徒。

於是她漸漸幻想自己就是那棵樹，
風支配著她，穿行於她青春的葉脈間，
支撐著她面向天空和那生意盎然的藍，
狂熱的雙手浸沒在陽光之中。
超脫腳下的青草和陰影，
她再無記憶，再無恐懼，再無希望。

TARK MAJOR

The lover's death, how regular
With lifting spring and starker
Vestiges of the sun that somehow
Filter in to us before we waken.

Not yet is there that heat and sober
Vivisection of more clamant air
That hands joined in the dark will answer
After the daily circuits of its glare.

It is the time of sundering . . .
Beneath the green silk counterpane
Her mound of undelivered life
Lies cool upon her—not yet pain.

And she will wake before you pass,
Scarcely aloud, beyond her door,

死板的大調

戀人之死,多麼規律
隨著振起的春和死板的
疏落陽光,不知不覺就
在我們睡醒前透了進來。

然而尚未透進來的是熱度還有
剖析空氣中嘈嚷的那分清醒
當旭光結束每日的周行
黑暗中緊握的手自會解釋答案。

該是別離的時候了⋯⋯
她仍未實現的生命
墳塚就在碧綠絲綢床單下
冷冷蓋覆著她── 痛苦卻未到來。

幾乎毫無聲息,在她門外,
你每步三階走下樓梯

And every third step down the stair
Until you reach the muffled floor—

Will laugh and call your name; while you
Still answering her faint good-byes,
Will find the street, only to look
At doors and stone with broken eyes.

Wake now, and note the lover's death.
Henceforth her memory is more
Than yours, in cries, in ecstasies
You cannot ever reach to share.

直到足踏鋪墊過的地板——
在你經過之前她將甦醒,

她將輕聲笑著呼喚你的名——當你
還在回應她氣若游絲的聲聲告別,
走上街去,只為用破碎的目光
再看一眼重門幽石。

醒來吧,記下戀人之死。
從此以後,她的記憶比你的
更多,在哭喊中,在狂喜中
你永遠都不得分享。

CHAPLINESQUE

We make our meek adjustments,
Contented with such random consolations
As the wind deposits
In slithered and too ample pockets.

For we can still love the world, who find
A famished kitten on the step, and know
Recesses for it from the fury of the street,
Or warm torn elbow coverts.

We will sidestep, and to the final smirk
Dally the doom of that inevitable thumb
That slowly chafes its puckered index toward us,
Facing the dull squint with what innocence
And what surprise!

And yet these fine collapses are not lies
More than the pirouettes of any pliant cane;

卓別林調調

我們溫順調整自己,
滿足於這般隨機的安慰
一如風沉進
滑溜且寬敞的口袋。

因為我們還是能愛這個世界——發現
臺階上一隻餓壞的小貓,知道
在街頭的狂亂中牠仍有棲身之處,
躲起來暖一暖磨破皮的肘。

我們會袖手旁觀,直到最後的假笑
拖延命定的厄運,拇指免不了
慢慢摩擦蜷向自己的食指,
面向那雙多麼天真又多麼驚訝
黯淡無神的瞇瞇眼。

然而比起那搭配巧杖的趾尖旋轉
這些難以察覺的崩解可不是虛言。

Our obsequies are, in a way, no enterprise.
We can evade you, and all else but the heart:
What blame to us if the heart live on.

The game enforces smirks; but we have seen
The moon in lonely alleys make
A grail of laughter of an empty ash can,
And through all sound of gaiety and quest
Have heard a kitten in the wilderness.

我們的弔唁,可以說,並非刻意為之。
我們可以逃避你逃避一切,但逃避不了心:
倘若心還活著,又有什麼好責備我們。

這場遊戲強迫假笑;不過我們都看過
明月把僻巷中的空垃圾桶
變成盛滿歡笑的聖杯,
而穿過所有的歡聲雷動與探幽索隱
我們都聽過茫茫荒野中的一隻小貓。

PASTORALE

No more violets,
And the year
Broken into smoky panels.
What woods remember now
Her calls, her enthusiasms.

That ritual of sap and leaves
The sun drew out,
Ends in this latter muffled
Bronze and brass. The wind
Takes rein.

If, dusty, I bear
An image beyond this
Already fallen harvest,
I can only query, "Fool—
Have you remembered too long;

田園曲

不再有紫羅蘭,
而年辰
已裂解成煙靄中的碎片。
樹林如今還記得的是
她的呼喚,她的熱情。

樹汁和樹葉的儀式
因太陽而萌發,
終結在後來悶住聲音的
青銅與黃銅之中。由風
接掌。

如果漫天塵土,而我
仍超脫已然凋落的豐收
胸臆自懷景象,
那我只能探問,「癡人——
你的追憶是否太過久遠;

Or was there too little said
For ease or resolution—
Summer scarcely begun
And violets,
A few picked, the rest dead?"

還是對於放下或者堅持
訴說得太少——
夏天還沒真正開始
而紫羅蘭,
有幾朵已採,而其餘凋殘?」

IN SHADOW

Out in the late amber afternoon,
Confused among chrysanthemums,
Her parasol, a pale balloon,
Like a waiting moon, in shadow swims.

Her furtive lace and misty hair
Over the garden dial distill
The sunlight,—then withdrawing, wear
Again the shadows at her will.

Gently yet suddenly, the sheen
Of stars inwraps her parasol.
She hears my step behind the green
Twilight, stiller than shadows, fall.

"Come, it is too late,—too late
To risk alone the light's decline:

在暗影中

琥珀色的傍晚,
混淆菊花叢間,
她的陽傘,蒼白的氣球,
像一輪等待的月,在暗影中漂游。

她晦密的蕾絲和迷濛的長髮
在花園的日晷上蒸餾
陽光——繼而提煉,終於
如她所願再次穿上暗影。

輕輕柔柔卻突如其來,群星的
輝光包裹她的陽傘。
她聽見我的腳步在黝綠的暮光
背後,比暗影更加靜默,降臨。

「來吧,已經太晚,——太晚了
別一個人冒著暮光褪去的危險:

Now has the evening long to wait,"—
But her own words are night's and mine.

還得等一段時間夜幕才會降臨,」——
而她的倩語屬於夜晚,也屬於我。

THE FERNERY

The lights that travel on her spectacles
Seldom, now, meet a mirror in her eyes.
But turning, as you may chance to lift a shade
Beside her and her fernery, is to follow
The zigzags fast around dry lips composed
To darkness through a wreath of sudden pain.

—So, while fresh sunlight splinters humid green
I have known myself a nephew to confusions
That sometimes take up residence and reign
In crowns less grey—O merciless tidy hair!

蕨圃

此刻,她眼鏡上游移的光線
難得把她的眼眸映成了明鏡。
然而轉眼,當你掀起
她蕨圃旁的門簾,剛好跟上的卻是
枯唇抖擂的起起落落,驟至的疼痛串起花環
在黑暗中平靜下來。

—— 所以當清新的陽光破解潮濕的綠意
我終於明白自己原來是困惑的子嗣
時而頭戴尚未轉為灰白的冠冕
深居其中統治——啊無情井然的白髮!

NORTH LABRADOR

A land of leaning ice
Hugged by plaster-grey arches of sky,
Flings itself silently
Into eternity.

"Has no one come here to win you,
Or left you with the faintest blush
Upon your glittering breasts?
Have you no memories, O Darkly Bright?"

Cold-hushed, there is only the shifting of moments
That journey toward no Spring—
No birth, no death, no time nor sun
In answer.

北拉布拉多

斜袤的寒冰之地,
被灰白穹頂的天空環抱,
靜靜投身
永恆之中。

「難道無人曾來此征服妳,
或者在妳耀眼的胸脯上
留下淡淡的紅暈?
難道妳毫無記憶,哦,黑暗的光明?」

因凜寒而寂寥,只有光陰流轉
朝向永遠不會到來的春天——
無生,無死,無時亦無日
回答。

REPOSE OF RIVERS

The willows carried a slow sound,
A sarabande the wind mowed on the mead.
I could never remember
That seething, steady leveling of the marshes
Till age had brought me to the sea.

Flags, weeds. And remembrance of steep alcoves
Where cypresses shared the noon's
Tyranny; they drew me into hades almost.
And mammoth turtles climbing sulphur dreams
Yielded, while sun-silt rippled them
Asunder . . .

How much I would have bartered! the black gorge
And all the singular nestings in the hills
Where beavers learn stitch and tooth.
The pond I entered once and quickly fled—
I remember now its singing willow rim.

河的長眠

柳樹帶著一縷悠緩的聲音,
風吹起薩拉班德舞曲刈著草地。
我始終記不起來
沼澤沸湧翻騰,又規律地平伏
直到歲月把我帶向大海。

旗幟,野草。還有記憶裡陡峭的林間僻靜之地
柏樹和正午的豔陽攜手
專制;他們幾乎把我拖進冥府。
巨大如猛獁象的海龜攀爬上硫磺色的夢境
當陽光的淤泥蕩漾,漣漪的波紋把牠們蕩為碎片
夢境也屈曲崩塌⋯⋯

我願意用多少代價交換啊!窈黑的峽谷
和山丘裡所有獨一無二的鳥窩
海狸在那裡學會築壩和啃囓。
我曾經踏進一回便匆匆逃離的池塘——
現在我記起來池塘邊緣是歌唱的柳樹。

And finally, in that memory all things nurse;
After the city that I finally passed
With scalding unguents spread and smoking darts
The monsoon cut across the delta
At gulf gates . . . There, beyond the dykes

I heard wind flaking sapphire, like this summer,
And willows could not hold more steady sound.

終於,萬物都在那記憶中滋養;
在我終於通過的城市之後
帶著滾燙的香膏和冒煙的箭矢
季風在海灣的入口
橫切三角洲而過……就在那裡,我聽見在堤壩的另一邊

吹過的風帶來片片落下的青玉,就像這個夏天,而柳樹再也無法保持更堅定不變的聲音。

PARAPHRASE

Of a steady winking beat between
Systole, diastole spokes-of-a-wheel
One rushing from the bed at night
May find the record wedged in his soul.

Above the feet the clever sheets
Lie guard upon the integers of life:
For what skims in between uncurls the toe,
Involves the hands in purposeless repose.

But from its bracket how can the tongue tell
When systematic morn shall sometime flood
The pillow—how desperate is the light
That shall not rouse, how faint the crow's cavil

As, when stunned in that antarctic blaze,
Your head, unrocking to a pulse, already

另一種說法

心臟收縮,心臟舒張像轉輪的輻條
之間閃爍的節拍規律而穩定
夜晚從床榻倉促起身的人
或許會發現紀錄就牢牢楔在靈魂之中。

機敏的床單蓋在雙腳之上
守護著生命的整數:
因為其間飛快掠過的東西會讓腳趾撐開拉直,
卻讓雙手陷入毫無目的的歇止。

但從生命的括弧裡舌頭怎麼分辨得出
什麼時候規律井然的早晨會氾濫
枕畔──晨光多麼渴望
卻無法喚人甦醒,報曉聲中的指責多麼微弱

就像在南極那烈焰中大為震驚之際,
你的頭顱,不隨脈搏振動,早已

Hallowed by air, posts a white paraphrase
Among bruised roses on the papered wall.

被空氣神聖化,在壁紙上傷痕累累的玫瑰之間張貼了白色的另一種說法。

POSSESSIONS

Witness now this trust! the rain
That steals softly direction
And the key, ready to hand—sifting
One moment in sacrifice (the direst)
Through a thousand nights the flesh
Assaults outright for bolts that linger
Hidden,—O undirected as the sky
That through its black foam has no eyes
For this fixed stone of lust . . .

Accumulate such moments to an hour:
Account the total of this trembling tabulation,
I know the screen, the distant flying taps
And stabbing medley that sways—
And the mercy, feminine, that stays
As though prepared.

擁有

點檢如今託交何在！雨
輕輕柔柔中盜走了方向
和觸手可及的那把鑰匙——
閃電在外頭徘徊而後隱匿
慾望肆無忌憚在夜晚來襲
從一千個這樣的夜晚
篩選出獻祭中（最危急存亡）
的片刻，——啊就如天空已失定向
透過黑色的泡沫看不清
如磐石穩固的慾念……

把這樣的片刻累積到一小時：
計算這份戰慄的列表總和，
我認得那篩子，遠處飄揚的輕拍聲，
搖曳的椎心樂曲集錦——
還有逗留在那
彷彿早就預備好的慈悲和陰柔。

And I, entering, take up the stone
As quiet as you can make a man . . .
In Bleecker Street, still trenchant in a void,
Wounded by apprehensions out of speech,
I hold it up against a disk of light—
I, turning, turning on smoked forking spires,
The city's stubborn lives, desires.

Tossed on these horns, who bleeding dies,
Lacks all but piteous admissions to be spilt
Upon the page whose blind sum finally burns
Record of rage and partial appetites.
The pure possession, the inclusive cloud
Whose heart is fire shall come,—the white wind raze
All but bright stones wherein our smiling plays.

而我，步入其中，安靜領受了磐石
你們可以讓人多安靜我就多安靜……
在布利克街，空洞虛無之中依舊咄咄逼人，
我被那莫可名狀的恐懼所傷，
於是高舉那磐石對著一輪光明——
我，轉呀轉，轉呀轉，在煙灰色的分岔尖塔上，
在這座城市執拗的眾生和慾念上。

輾轉在這些尖角之上，流血至死的人
一無所有只剩下哀憐的供認：自己已在
紙頁上四分五裂，而盲目的總和
終究焚燬憤怒和破碎慾念的紀錄。
純粹的擁有，包容的雲
中心是火焰，終將到來，——白色的風夷
平一切
只剩下光明的磐石，裡面播放著我們的笑。

LACHRYMAE CHRISTI

Whitely, while benzene
Rinsings from the moon
Dissolve all but the windows of the mills
(Inside the sure machinery
Is still
And curdled only where a sill
Sluices its one unyielding smile)

Immaculate venom binds
The fox's teeth, and swart
Thorns freshen on the year's
First blood. From flanks unfended,
Twanged red perfidies of spring
Are trillion on the hill.

And the nights opening
Chant pyramids,—
Anoint with innocence,—recall

基督之淚

那是一片白,當月光下
苯的漂洗
溶解了工廠窗戶以外的一切
(而穩健的機器內部
闃寂靜止
窗臺奔瀉一抹不肯屈服的微笑
是唯一凝結的地方)

純潔無瑕的毒液纏繞
狐狸的齒,惡毒的刺
在今年的第一滴血上
精神煥發。從不設防的脅腹,
彈撥春天的紅色背叛
其數億兆京垓迴盪山間。

而夜的開場白
歌頌金字塔,——
膏以純真,——回想起

To music and retrieve what perjuries
Had galvanized the eyes.

                While chime
Beneath and all around
Distilling clemencies,—worms'
Inaudible whistle, tunneling
Not penitence
But song, as these
Perpetual fountains, vines,—

Thy Nazarene and tinder eyes.

(Let sphinxes from the ripe
Borage of death have cleared my tongue
Once and again; vermin and rod
No longer bind. Some sentient cloud
Of tears flocks through the tendoned loam:
Betrayed stones slowly speak.)

樂聲也在眼中重新得見
虛誓帶來的激勵。

    鐘樂
來自地底和八方
蒸餾出仁慈寬厚，——而蟲蟻
那不可聞的吟鳴，暗自鑿通的
並非痛悔
而是讚詩，一如
不舍晝夜的清泉和四時長青的葡萄樹，
——

祢納匝肋人的眼就是火種。

（從熟成的死亡琉璃苣中
釋放斯芬克斯，使我舌得以潔淨
一次又一次；再不受
蟲害和荊杖的束縛。淚的雲朵也有知覺
於是穿越筋脈相連的沃土群集而至：
眾叛親離的石緩緩吐露心跡。）

Names peeling from Thine eyes
And their undimming lattices of flame,
Spell out in palm and pain
Compulsion of the year, O Nazarene.

Lean long from sable, slender boughs,
Unstanched and luminous. And as the nights
Strike from Thee perfect spheres,
Lift up in lilac-emerald breath the grail
Of earth again—

Thy face
From charred and riven stakes, O
Dionysus, Thy
Unmangled target smile.

名號從祢眼底
從永不黯淡的烈火格柵後逐一剝落,
在掌心上在痛苦中詳述
時代難以抗拒的衝動,哦納匝肋人。

長倚烏黑纖細的樹枝,
血流不止卻散發光輝。而當夜幕
從祢完美無暇的天空降臨,
在紫碧氤氳之中
大地的聖杯再次高舉——

在燒焦劈裂的火刑柱上
祢的面容,哦
戴奧尼索斯,祢那
毫髮無傷的微笑。

基督之淚

PASSAGE

Where the cedar leaf divides the sky
I heard the sea.
In sapphire arenas of the hills
I was promised an improved infancy.

Sulking, sanctioning the sun,
My memory I left in a ravine,—
Casual louse that tissues the buck-wheat,
Aprons rocks, congregates pears
In moonlit bushels
And wakens alleys with a hidden cough.

Dangerously the summer burned
(I had joined the entrainments of the wind).
The shadows of boulders lengthened my back:
In the bronze gongs of my cheeks
The rain dried without odour.

時光通道

雪松葉劃分天空的畛域
在那裡我聽見海。
群丘環抱而成的青玉色競技場
應許了我更好的一段孩提。

悶氣鬱結的時候,就讚許太陽,
我把回憶就遺留在深谷,——
偶有一鄙夫包裹起蕎麥,
給礫石穿上圍裙,把梨子聚集成堆
放進月光下的籃子裡
然後用隱藏的咳嗽喚醒里巷。

夏日熊熊燃燒危險而不安
(而我也是隨風而逝的一分子了)
巨石的陰影拉長我的背:
我的臉頰就是銅鑼
雨水在裡面乾去不帶一絲氣味。

"It is not long, it is not long;
See where the red and black
Vine-stanchioned valleys—": but the wind
Died speaking through the ages that you know
And bug, chimney-sooted heart of man!
So was I turned about and back, much as your smoke
Compiles a too well-known biography.

The evening was a spear in the ravine
That throve through very oak. And had I walked
The dozen particular decimals of time?
Touching an opening laurel, I found
A thief beneath, my stolen book in hand.

"Why are you back here—smiling an iron coffin?"
"To argue with the laurel," I replied:
"Am justified in transience, fleeing
Under the constant wonder of your eyes—."

He closed the book. And from the Ptolemies
Sand troughed us in a glittering, abyss.

「這不算長,這不算長;
看看那些有紅色和黑色
葡萄藤蔓撐起的山谷──」:透過你知曉的時代
病菌,還有煙囪煤灰燻黑的人心
風傾訴著,但如今已不再吹拂!
你的濃濃黑煙編纂成一本著名的傳記,
於是心也燻黑了的我轉身回來。

夜晚是深谷中的一支長矛,
透過那株橡樹成長茁壯。我是否已然逐一
行經時光的那許多片段?
觸摸敞開的月桂樹,我發現
小偷躲在下面,手裡就握著我被偷走的書。

「你為什麼回來這裡──板著臉微笑?」
「回來和月桂樹爭論,」我回答:
「你眼底的驚異未嘗停歇,
這一瞬間你的遁逃便情有可原──。」

他闔上書。從托勒密時代
光彩奪目的深淵,沙把我們困在那槽裡。

A serpent swam a vertex to the sun
—On unpaced beaches leaned its tongue and drummed.
What fountains did I hear? What icy speeches?
Memory, committed to the page, had broke.

蛇頂著頭游向太陽
——把舌頭靠在無人踏足的海灘上敲打著。
我聽到的是什麼泉源？是什麼冰冷的言詞？
記憶，交付給書頁，已經四分五裂。

THE WINE MENAGERIE

Invariably when wine redeems the sight,
Narrowing the mustard scansions of the eyes,
A leopard ranging always in the brow
Asserts a vision in the slumbering gaze.

Then glozening decanters that reflect the street
Wear me in crescents on their bellies. Slow
Applause flows into liquid cynosures:
—I am conscripted to their shadows' glow.

Against the imitation onyx wainscoting
(Painted emulsion of snow, eggs, yarn, coal, manure)
Regard the forceps of the smile that takes her.
Percussive sweat is spreading to his hair. Mallets,
Her eyes, unmake an instant of the world . . .

醇酒動物園

每當美酒讓視力得救,
把眼光的掃視斂縮在芥子大小,
總有一頭花豹遊走眉宇之間
在惺忪的凝眸中體現一幅幻象。

然後反映街景光影的酒瓶
把我也映進了瓶腹上的月弧。
液態的星辰指引喝采的流瀉:
—— 眾星陰影的光輝也將我徵召而去。

倚靠著仿縞瑪瑙的壁板
(那像雪、蛋、紗、煤和肥料的乳濁感是畫出來的)
她凝視著那如鑷子般把她夾走的笑容。
汗水像打擊樂器的節拍在他的髮間蔓延開來。像木槌,
她的眼,拆解了世界的那一瞬間。

What is it in this heap the serpent pries—
Whose skin, facsimile of time, unskeins
Octagon, sapphire transepts round the eyes;
—From whom some whispered carillon assures
Speed to the arrow into feathered skies?

Sharp to the window-pane guile drags a face,
And as the alcove of her jealousy recedes
An urchin who has left the snow
Nudges a cannister across the bar
While August meadows somewhere clasp his brow.

Each chamber, transept, coins some squint,
Remorseless line, minting their separate wills—
Poor streaked bodies wreathing up and out,
Unwitting the stigma that each turn repeals:
Between black tusks the roses shine!

在這層層疊疊之中蛇究竟想窺探些什麼——
是誰的膚觸，時光的摹本，鬆開
紡紗機上絞好的綹，眼瞼四周青玉色的袖廊；
——低鳴的編鐘又是從誰的嘴裡允諾給予飛箭
速度衝向羽毛做成的天空？

窗框的玻璃前驟現一張因著狡詐而拖拉過來
的臉龐，
而當她靈魂深處的妒意漸漸褪去
離雪而去的淘氣孩子
輕推著茶罐穿越沙洲而來
八月的草坪差不多就是在這個時候攢緊他的
眉頭。

一間間廳堂，袖廊，造就某種側睨，
冷血的線條，鑄就各自的意志——
可憐的裸身盤旋上升離去，
每一次轉身都在不知不覺間抹去汙名：
玫瑰在黑色的獠牙間閃耀光芒！

醇酒動物園

New thresholds, new anatomies! Wine talons
Build freedom up about me and distill
This competence—to travel in a tear
Sparkling alone, within another's will.

Until my blood dreams a receptive smile
Wherein new purities are snared; where chimes
Before some flame of gaunt repose a shell
Tolled once, perhaps, by every tongue in hell.
—Anguished, the wit that cries out of me:

"Alas,— these frozen billows of your skill!
Invent new dominoes of love and bile . . .
Ruddy, the tooth implicit of the world
Has followed you. Though in the end you know
And count some dim inheritance of sand,
How much yet meets the treason of the snow.

新的開端,新的身體結構!酒的爪
在我周遭集結自由繼而萃取
這能力的精華——在一滴獨自閃閃發光
的淚珠裡旅行,儘管是在別人的意志之中。

直到我的血夢見一抹敞開胸懷的微笑,
新生的純潔在那裡落入圈套;那裡的管鐘
在幾簇憔悴的火焰之前,或許用上地獄裡的
每一條舌頭
終於讓那一度被剝削殆盡的空殼憩止。
——清醒的理智感受極度的苦痛,從我內
心哭喊出聲來:

「嗚呼,你的熟巧如冰濤襲來!
用情愛和忿鬱創造出新的骨牌……
該死,這塵世含蓄的齒
已經在你身後伺機咬下。儘管最後你會知道
並且細數沙岸上幽微的遺跡,
迄今有多少符合雪的背叛。

"Rise from the dates and crumbs. And walk away,
Stepping ver Holofernes' shins—
Beyond the wall, whose severed head floats by
With Baptist John's. Their whispering begins.

"—And fold your exile on your back again;
Petrushka's valentine pivots on its pin."

「從棗子和麵包屑裡站起身來。一走了之，
踩敖羅斐乃[6]的脛骨而去──
在牆的另一邊，他的斷頭隨著洗者若翰[7]的，
齊漂浮而過。他們開始竊竊私語。
「── 背上你的行囊再次離鄉背井；
彼得魯什卡[8]的情人在唱針上旋轉。」

RECITATIVE

Regard the capture here, O Janus-faced,
As double as the hands that twist this glass.
Such eyes at search or rest you cannot see;
Reciting pain or glee, how can you bear!

Twin shadowed halves: the breaking second holds
In each the skin alone, and so it is
I crust a plate of vibrant mercury
Borne cleft to you, and brother in the half.

Inquire this much-exacting fragment smile,
Its drums and darkest blowing leaves ignore,—
Defer though, revocation of the tears
That yield attendance to one crucial sign.

Look steadily—how the wind feasts and spins
The brain's disk shivered against lust. Then watch
While darkness, like an ape's face, falls away,

宣敘調

注意這一段扣人心弦的地方,正反兩面[9],
像扭曲這面鏡子的雙手左右不一。
你看不出來這樣的眼眸是在尋覓或者歇息;
宣敘痛楚或者歡愉,你怎能承受!

影子遮蔽的半邊自成一對:破碎的一半
獨自緊抓著另一半的外皮,也確實如此
震顫的那盤水銀帶給你裂解
所以我結其為鏡,伴你在這半邊。

向至為嚴苛的破碎微笑探問,
其鼓聲和黝黑飛揚的樹葉卻都不理會,——
儘管延遲了,卻撤除了
那引發關鍵徵象的眼淚。

請從容觀望——風如何盛情款待並轉動
腦中因慾望而顫抖的唱盤。然後看清楚,
當黑暗——如猩猩的黑臉——消散,

And gradually white buildings answer day.

Let the same nameless gulf beleaguer us—
Alike suspend us from atrocious sums
Built floor by floor on shafts of steel that grant
The plummet heart, like Absalom, no stream.

The highest tower,—let her ribs palisade
Wrenched gold of Nineveh;—yet leave the tower.
The bridge swings over salvage, beyond wharves;
A wind abides the ensign of your will . . .

In alternating bells have you not heard
All hours clapped dense into a single stride?
Forgive me for an echo of these things,
And let us walk through time with equal pride.

漸漸有白屋答覆白晝的呼喚。

就讓同一片無名的海灣將我們圍困——
同樣也將我們從芸芸凡胎中吊掛出來
因他們在鋼樑之上搭建層層高樓
使心如鉛錘孤懸，如阿貝沙隆[10]，不再湧流。

最高的塔樓，——讓她的拱肋護衛
從尼尼微[11]掠奪的黃金；——還是棄塔樓而去吧。
碼頭之外，橋樑在前來營救的隊伍上方擺動；
風恆存於你意志的旗幟中……

在交替的鐘聲中難道你未曾聽見
所有歲月被緊壓進邁開的一大步？
原諒我把這些舊事一提再提，
就讓我們懷抱同樣的驕傲在時光中漫步。

FOR THE MARRIAGE OF FAUSTUS AND HELEN

"And so we may arrive by Talmud skill
And profane Greek to raise the building up
Of Helen's house against the Ismaelite,
King of Thogarma, and his habergeons
Brimstony, blue and fiery; and the force
Of King A baddon, and the beast of Cittim;
Which Rabbi David Kimchi, Onkelos,
And Aben Ezra do interpret Rome."
—THE ALCHEMIST

I

The mind has shown itself at times
Too much the baked and labeled dough
Divided by accepted multitudes.
Across the stacked partitions of the day—

為浮士德與海倫成婚而作

「如此一來我們可以憑藉《塔木德》裡的技巧
和俚俗的希臘語建立起
海倫的房舍,對抗依巿瑪耳族人,
托加爾瑪的國王,還有他如地獄硫磺如藍焰如烈火
的短鎧甲軍團;以及阿巴頓王
的軍隊,和基提姆的野獸;
這是大衛・金齊拉比、翁克洛斯,
和阿本・埃茲拉詮釋下的羅馬。」
——《煉金術士》(1610)。

I

心靈偶爾表現出自己原有的樣子
大多時候卻像烘烤塑形後貼上標籤的麵團
被默許的芸芸眾生分食。
越過白天裡的層層隔閡——

Across the memoranda, baseball scores,
The stenographic smiles and stock quotations
Smutty wings flash out equivocations.

The mind is brushed by sparrow wings;
Numbers, rebuffed by asphalt, crowd
The margins of the day, accent the curbs,
Convoying divers dawns on every corner
To druggist, barber and tobacconist,
Until the graduate opacities of evening
Take them away as suddenly to somewhere
Virginal perhaps, less fragmentary, cool.

> *There is the world dimensional for*
> *those untwisted by the love of things*
> *irreconcilable . . .*

And yet, suppose some evening I forgot
The fare and transfer, yet got by that way
Without recall,—lost yet poised in traffic.

越過備忘錄,越過棒球的比分,
越過速成的微笑還有股票報價單
煤煙燻黑的羽翼閃耀出模稜兩可的話語。

麻雀的羽翼輕拂心靈;
編號,被柏油路面冷落,擠滿
白天的邊緣,凸顯路緣石的存在,
在每一個轉角護送不同的曙光
去藥房老闆、理髮師和菸草商那裡,
直到漸濃的濁晦在傍晚
突然把他們帶到某個
或許是純潔無垢,沒有那麼破碎,而更冷
靜的地方。

> 愛上互不相容的事物
> 那些人因此得以解放
> 有一種世界的維度只屬於他們……

不過假設某個晚上我忘記
車資跟換車,卻在不經意間
走上那條路,——在車水馬龍中迷路卻泰
然自若。

Then I might find your eyes across an aisle,
Still flickering with those prefigurations—
Prodigal, yet uncontested now,
Half-riant before the jerky window frame.

There is some way, I think, to touch
Those hands of yours that count the nights
Stippled with pink and green advertisements.
And now, before its arteries turn dark
I would have you meet this bartered blood.
Imminent in his dream, none better knows
The white wafer cheek of love, or offers words
Lightly as moonlight on the eaves meets snow.

然後隔著走道我可能會發現妳的眼裡，
依舊閃爍著那些預兆──
曾經不知凡幾，如今卻無人爭搶，
半含著笑意，在停停動動的窗框前。

粉紅和綠色的廣告點綴夜晚
我想一定有什麼方法，可以觸碰
妳細數夜晚的那雙手。
而現在，在動脈變黑之前
我要讓妳看看這做為交換的鮮血。
在他的夢裡沒有人會更熟悉，那即將浮現的
一如聖餐餅白皙的愛的臉頰，也沒有人能更輕柔地
訴說話語，一如迎接白雪的屋簷上的月光。

Reflective conversion of all things
At your deep blush, when ecstasies thread
The limbs and belly, when rainbows spread
Impinging on the throat and sides . . .
Inevitable, the body of the world
Weeps in inventive dust for the hiatus
That winks above it, bluet in your breasts.

The earth may glide diaphanous to death;
But if I lift my arms it is to bend
To you who turned away once, Helen, knowing
The press of troubled hands, too alternate
With steel and soil to hold you endlessly.
I meet you, therefore, in that eventual flame
You found in final chains, no captive then
Beyond their million brittle, bloodshot eyes;
White, through white cities passed on to assume
That world which comes to each of us alone.

映照在妳的赭頰上
萬物因而轉變,當狂喜穿過
四肢與肚腹,當彩虹延展
撞擊在喉頭與脅肋⋯⋯
在創造的塵土中
世界的軀體為眨閃於其上的裂縫而哭泣,
避不開,妳胸口綻放的藍色花朵。

大地可能輕薄透明滑向死亡;
但如果我高舉雙臂伸向
曾經轉身離去的妳,海倫,妳認得
混亂不安的雙手的緊抱,因與鋼鐵和泥土
頻繁交替所以無法永無止境擁抱妳。
妳在最後的束縛中尋覓,覓得的烈焰
是我因此與妳相遇之處,從此我們就不再為
他們無數冷淡的布滿血絲的眼眸所俘虜;
潔白,穿越一座座潔白的城市接著
把分別來到妳我面前的世界據為己有。

Accept a lone eye riveted to your plane,
Bent axle of devotion along companion ways
That beat, continuous, to hourless days—
One inconspicuous, glowing orb of praise.

接受孤寂的眼神牢牢盯著妳的飛機,
忠誠的輪軸在相伴的一路上持續不斷跳動
屈服於沒有時間的日子——
那是一顆不引人側目,但灼熱發光的讚美之球。

II

Brazen hypnotics glitter here;
Glee shifts from foot to foot,
Magnetic to their tremulo.
This crashing opera bouffe,
Blest excursion! this ricochet
From roof to roof—
Know, Olympians, we are breathless
While nigger cupids scour the stars!

A thousand light shrugs balance us
Through snarling hails of melody.
White shadows slip across the floor
Splayed like cards from a loose hand;
Rhythmic ellipses lead into canters
Until somewhere a rooster banters.

Greet naïvely—yet intrepidly
New soothings, new amazements
That cornets introduce at every turn—

II

青銅色的催眠劑在這裡閃耀；
歡快的感覺從這一腳換到那一腳，
被雙腳顫動時的那股磁力吸引著。
這場嘰嘎作響的喜歌劇，
是段至福的遠足！反射彈跳
從一片屋頂到另外一片──
當黑人丘比特在星星間穿行搜索，
奧林匹斯諸神知道我們屏氣凝神！

我們輕輕聳肩千次以保持平衡
穿過一陣陣旋律咆哮的歡呼。
白色的影子在地板上滑行，
就像鬆開了手散落一地的牌；
有韻律的答答答化作策馬慢跑
直到某處的一隻公雞鬧著說笑。

短號在每個轉角引見
新的慰藉，新的驚奇
天真地迎接──卻毫無畏懼──

And you may fall downstairs with me
With perfect grace and equanimity.
Or, plaintively scud past shores
Where, by strange harmonic laws
All relatives, serene and cool,
Sit rocked in patent armchairs.

O, I have known metallic paradises
Where cuckoos clucked to finches
Above the deft catastrophes of drums.
While titters hailed the groans of death
Beneath gyrating awnings I have seen
The incunabula of the divine grotesque.
This music has a reassuring way.

The siren of the springs of guilty song—
Let us take her on the incandescent wax
Striated with nuances nervosities
That we are heir to: she is still so young,
She cannot frown upon her as she smiles,
Dipping here in this cultivated storm
Among slim skaters of the gardened skies.

你可能會身懷完美的優雅與沉著自若
跟我一起摔下樓梯。
又或者，滿懷憂悒疾掠過海岸
在那裡，根據奇異的和諧法則
所有親屬，安詳而冷靜，
坐在專有的扶手椅上搖啊搖。

哦，我知道有好幾座金屬的樂園
熟練的災難結局隨鼓聲而來
在那之上有布穀咯咯叫喚雀鳥。
就當嬉笑怒罵為死亡的呻吟喝采
在迴旋的涼篷下我看到
搖籃中神聖的怪誕即將萌生。
這音樂就是有方法教人心安。

賽蓮在罪惡之泉上美聲歌唱──
讓我們用熾熱的蠟封耳以抗
細微的差異和神經交織成蠟上的橫紋
我們本就是這蠟的子嗣：她依然如此青春，
浸身於此優雅的風暴
廁身於百花天空中輕盈的飛仙
當她嫣然一笑我們又何能蹙額皺眉。

III

Capped arbiter of beauty in this street
That narrows darkly into motor dawn,—
You, here beside me, delicate ambassador
Of intricate slain numbers that arise
In whispers, naked of steel;

                      religious gunman!
Who faithfully, yourself, will fall too soon,
And in other ways than as the wind settles
On the sixteen thrifty bridges of the city:
Let us unbind our throats of fear and pity.

                      We even,
Who drove speediest destruction
In corymbulous formations of mechanics,—
Who hurried the hill breezes, spouting malice
Plangent over meadows, and looked down
On rifts of torn and empty houses
Like old women with teeth unjubilant
That waited faintly, briefly and in vain:

III

美的仲裁者戴著帽在這條
黑暗中朝向汽車的黎明收束而去的街,──
被扼殺的數字錯綜複雜在私語中
浮現,毫無鋼鐵的遮蔽
此刻我身旁的妳,是其嬌貴的使者;
　　　　　　　　虔誠的槍手!
惓惓深摯的妳自己,也必將很快沉落,
而以其他不同的方式如風安身
在城市的十六座絡繹的大橋上:
就讓我們鬆開自己恐懼和憐憫的喉頭。

　　　　　　　　我們甚至,
在機械的傘狀花序結構之中
驅動最迅速的毀滅,──
我們催促山間微風,滔滔噴射惡意
在草地上悲切哀鳴,並俯瞰
崩碎和空蕩房舍的裂縫
就像滿口爛牙愁鬱鬱的老婦
虛弱,短促,徒然地等待:

We know, eternal gunman, our flesh remembers
The tensile boughs, the nimble blue plateaus,
The mounted, yielding cities of the air!

That saddled sky that shook down vertical
Repeated play of fire—no hypogeum
Of wave or rock was good against one hour.
We did not ask for that, but have survived,
And will persist to speak again before
All stubble streets that have not curved
To memory, or known the ominous lifted arm
That lowers down the arc of Helen's brow
To saturate with blessing and dismay.

A goose, tobacco and cologne—
Three winged and gold-shod prophecies of heaven,
The lavish heart shall always have to leaven
And spread with bells and voices, and atone
The abating shadows of our conscript dust.

永恆的槍手,我們知道自己的肉軀還記得
延展拉伸的樹枝,翩然的藍色高原,
凌空湧現其形千變萬化的天空之城!

套著鞍韉的天空抖落垂直
反覆搖曳的火光——沒有任何
波濤或巖石的地下陵寢能與時間抗衡。
我們雖未求全,然卻倖以身免,
在——只剩根荓的街道還未朝記憶的方向
彎曲,或猶未識那高舉預示不祥的手臂
讓海倫的眉弓低沉
浸潤於天惠與沮喪
之前——將堅持再一次盡言。

一隻雁,煙草和古龍水——
三則乘著翅翼踏金蹄鐵而來的天堂預言,
揮霍的心永遠需要發酵
繼而敷抹以鈴聲與萬籟,償贖
我們被徵召而去的塵土中漸趨虛弱的身影。

為浮士德與海倫成婚而作

Anchises' navel, dripping of the sea,—
The hands Erasmus dipped in gleaming tides,
Gathered the voltage of blown blood and vine;
Delve upward for the new and scattered wine,
O brother-thief of time, that we recall.
Laugh out the meager penance of their days
Who dare not share with us the breath released,
The substance drilled and spent beyond repair
For golden, or the shadow of gold hair.

Distinctly praise the years, whose volatile
Blamed bleeding hands extend and thresh the height
The imagination spans beyond despair,
Outpacing bargain, vocable and prayer.

安凱西斯的臍,是海的水滴,——
伊拉斯謨的手浸入閃閃發光的潮汐,
萃聚來自膨脹的血滴和葡萄藤的電壓;
向上方求索我們還能回想起稀落四散的
新釀葡萄酒,哦,時光盜賊我的手足。
對他們在年歲裡微薄的痛悔放聲談笑
卻不敢與我們分享已宣洩的氣息,
那些被鑽穿和耗盡而無法再因金色,
或是金髮的陰影而修復的物質。

無疑要讚美歲月,那喜怒無常
千夫所指的淌血雙手延展又反覆推敲出高度
使想像力得以跨越於絕望之上,
超前於買賣、語音和禱告。

AT MELVILLE'S TOMB

Often beneath the wave, wide from this ledge
The dice of drowned men's bones he saw bequeath
An embassy. Their numbers as he watched,
Beat on the dusty shore and were obscured.

And wrecks passed without sound of bells,
The calyx of death's bounty giving back
A scattered chapter, livid hieroglyph,
The portent wound in corridors of shells.

Then in the circuit calm of one vast coil,
Its lashings charmed and malice reconciled,
Frosted eyes there were that lifted altars;
And silent answers crept across the stars.

Compass, quadrant and sextant contrive
No farther tides . . . High in the azure steeps

在梅爾維爾墓前

常常在波濤之下,在距離這暗礁遠處
他看見波臣遺骨磋磨成骰子貽垂為後世的
使臣。骰子拍擊滿布塵埃的海岸,
當他定睛一看點數已漫漶難解。

失事船舶殘骸飄過,再無船鐘聲響,
沉沒的漩渦是死亡貽贈的花萼,回報以
零落的篇章,青灰色的象形祕文,
凶兆在海螺的迴廊間縈迴屈曲。

在巨大的迴圈中環行的是股風平浪靜,
凶兆的喝斥令人陶醉而其怨惡令人甘心,
死白的眼好似覆以霜雪就是升起的祭壇;
而沉默的回答不覺間蠕蠕穿越星辰而來。

羅盤,四分儀和六分儀已無法謀劃
更遠的潮汐……在碧空那樣高聳的地方

Monody shall not wake the mariner.
This fabulous shadow only the sea keeps.

輓歌已喚不醒水手。
只剩蒼海還留存傳說的蹤影。

VOYAGES

I

Above the fresh ruffles of the surf
Bright striped urchins flay each other with sand.
They have contrived a conquest for shell shucks,
And their fingers crumble fragments of baked weed
Gaily digging and scattering.

And in answer to their treble interjections
The sun beats lightning on the waves,
The waves fold thunder on the sand;
And could they hear me I would tell them:

O brilliant kids, frisk with your dog,
Fondle your shells and sticks, bleached
By time and the elements; but there is a line

遠航

I

海浪激起新的波紋,稍高的地方
穿著亮色條紋的頑皮孩子互丟沙子嬉鬧扭打。
他們謀劃了一場貝殼的掠奪大計,
用手指戳爛曬乾的海草碎片
興高采烈地掏挖撒了滿地。

為了回應他們尖聲的喧嚷
太陽在波浪上擊出閃電,
波浪在沙灘上裹住雷鳴;
如果他們能聽見我那我會告訴他們:

聰穎的孩子啊,和你們的狗狗歡躍蹦跳,
摩挲你們那已被光陰和乾坤元行褪成白色的
貝殼和枝條;可是有一條線

You must not cross nor ever trust beyond it
Spry cordage of your bodies to caresses
Too lichen-faithful from too wide a breast.
The bottom of the sea is cruel.

你們絕對不要跨越,也永遠不要把你們身
體矯健的繩索
從太寬廣的胸臆託付給那條線之外
太像地衣般堅貞附著的愛撫。
海的深處是殘酷的。

II

—And yet this great wink of eternity,
Of rimless floods, unfettered leewardings,
Samite sheeted and processioned where
Her undinal vast belly moonward bends,
Laughing the wrapt inflections of our love;

Take this Sea, whose diapason knells
On scrolls of silver snowy sentences,
The sceptred terror of whose sessions rends
As her demeanors motion well or ill,
All but the pieties of lovers' hands.

And onward, as bells off San Salvador
Salute the crocus lustres of the stars,
In these poinsettia meadows of her tides,—

II

——然而無邊無際的洪流，無拘無束的背風，
以永恆的姿態深深眨了這一下眼，
錦繡鋪展蔓延之處
她遼闊的肚腹有如水的女神溫蒂妮朝月的方向而去
嘲笑我們愛情的纏繞曲折：

乘著這片海吧，銀白如雪的樂句寫滿卷軸
海的主旋律於其上鳴起喪鐘報凶的強音，
當她翩翩的風度時而和睦時而險惡地律動
她的演奏中有恐懼恃權稱王撕扯一切，
除了戀人手中緊握的虔誠。

前行未歇，當聖薩爾瓦多岸際的鐘聲
向閃耀著番紅花色光澤的星辰致意，
她的潮汐在片片聖誕紅的原野上去還，——

Adagios of islands, O my Prodigal,
Complete the dark confessions her veins spell.

Mark how her turning shoulders wind the hours,
And hasten while her penniless rich palms
Pass superscription of bent foam and wave,—
Hasten, while they are true,—sleep, death, desire,
Close round one instant in one floating flower.

Bind us in time, O Seasons clear, and awe.
O minstrel galleons of Carib fire,
Bequeath us to no earthly shore until
Is answered in the vortex of our grave
The seal's wide spindrift gaze toward paradise.

這是島嶼的慢板,哦我的浪子,
完成了她用血管拼寫而成的黑暗告解。

留意她轉動的肩膀如何使光陰蜿蜒,
又如何催促光陰當她一貧如洗卻肥沃豐饒的手掌
穿透彎曲的泡沫和波浪成就的題銘,——
催促著,就當光陰仍確鑿之際,—— 睡眠,死亡,渴望,
在一朵漂浮的花裡周而復始結束一個瞬間。

哦分明的四季,請把我們束縛在時間與敬畏之中。
哦加勒比之火的吟遊大帆船隊,
直到海豹在浪花飛沫中朝向天堂的凝視
在我們墓穴的漩渦中得到回應之前
請不要把我們遺贈給塵世的海岸。

III

Infinite consanguinity it bears—
This tendered theme of you that light
Retrieves from sea plains where the sky
Resigns a breast that every wave enthrones;
While ribboned water lanes I wind
Are laved and scattered with no stroke
Wide from your side, whereto this hour
The sea lifts, also, reliquary hands.

And so, admitted through black swollen gates
That must arrest all distance otherwise,—
Past whirling pillars and lithe pediments,
Light wrestling there incessantly with light,
Star kissing star through wave on wave unto
Your body rocking!
          and where death, if shed,

III

海負載無邊無際的親緣──
天空在海的平原上放棄了
每一道波浪都尊奉為王的胸懷
光從那裡復得你馴柔的主旋律；
我在緞帶似的水道中迂迴
沒有突如其來的沖擊但卻潰散之際
在你身側遙遠之處，朝向此時此刻
海也高舉聖物檯般的雙手。

就這樣，被允許穿過重重黑色臃腫的
必然會用其他不同方式阻斷所有距離的柵
門，──
經過迴旋的廊柱和柔軟的山形楣飾，
在那裡光線和光線交纏扭打沒有停歇，
星子親吻星子遍及波浪之上的波浪直到
你擺蕩的身軀！
　　　　　在那裡死亡，如果可以擺脫，

Presumes no carnage, but this single change,—
Upon the steep floor flung from dawn to dawn
The silken skilled transmemberment of song;

Permit me voyage, love, into your hands . . .

不再擅自放肆殺戮,唯獨只有這單一的變
化,——
絲綢般柔軟光潔的諳練歌聲拆解記憶變形
重組
在陡峭的地面從黎明直奔下一個黎明;

請許我遠航,吾愛,進入你的雙手……

IV

Whose counted smile of hours and days, suppose
I know as spectrum of the sea and pledge
Vastly now parting gulf on gulf of wings
Whose circles bridge, I know, (from palms to the severe
Chilled albatross's white immutability)
No stream of greater love advancing now
Than, singing, this mortality alone
Through clay aflow immortally to you.

All fragrance irrefragably, and claim
Madly meeting logically in this hour
And region that is ours to wreathe again,
Portending eyes and lips and making told
The chancel port and portion of our June—

Shall they not stem and close in our own steps
Bright staves of flowers and quills today as I
Must first be lost in fatal tides to tell?

IV

是誰的微笑計算著時時刻刻日日夜夜,料想
我知道答案,當海與誓言的光譜如今
遼遠地別離了羽翼的疊疊海灣,
是誰的環環相連,我知道答案,(從棕櫚樹乃至
凜冽信天翁白色的恆定不變)
歌唱著,必朽的生命藉由塵土
獨自用不朽的方式流淌向你
如今已無川流負載較之更偉大的愛洶湧前奔。

所有的芳馨無可辯駁地,且狂放地
宣稱在屬於我們的此時此地
再次繚繞為花環是合乎邏輯的相遇,
預示了眼眸和嘴唇並且告知
聖壇港口所在和我們六月命運的定數——

鮮花和羽毛筆下生氣勃勃的詩句
今日我必然先迷失於致命的潮汐才能吟誦
難道就不會在我們自己的腳步中堵截閉隔?

In signature of the incarnate word
The harbor shoulders to resign in mingling
Mutual blood, transpiring as foreknown
And widening noon within your breast for gathering
All bright insinuations that my years have caught
For islands where must lead inviolably
Blue latitudes and levels of your eyes,—

In this expectant, still exclaim receive
The secret oar and petals of all love.

彼此的血液,一如已然預知地那樣蒸騰著
在文字化為實形體現的簽名之中
海港肩負重責聽命將血液融合
並在你的胸臆間使正午擴展方得以匯聚
我在歲月中為諸島拾得的所有昭彰的影射
那諸島亦必然不容違背地導引著
你眼中蔚藍的緯度和水平線,——

在這滿懷盼望卻靜止無聲的驚呼中迎接
所有愛的祕密船槳和花瓣。

V

Meticulous, past midnight in clear rime,
Infrangible and lonely, smooth as though cast
Together in one merciless white blade—
The bay estuaries fleck the hard sky limits.

—As if too brittle or too clear to touch!
The cables of our sleep so swiftly filed,
Already hang, shred ends from remembered stars.
One frozen trackless smile . . . What words
Can strangle this deaf moonlight? For we

Are overtaken. Now no cry, no sword
Can fasten or deflect this tidal wedge,
Slow tyranny of moonlight, moonlight loved
And changed . . . "There's

Nothing like this in the world," you say,
Knowing I cannot touch your hand and look
Too, into that godless cleft of sky

V

小心翼翼,午夜過後晶瑩的霜淞中,
堅不可摧又形單影隻,光滑得彷彿澆鑄
合一成為一把冷酷無情的雪白利刃——
海灣的河口斑駁了天空堅硬的邊界。

——彷彿太易脆裂或太過清澈而不能觸摸!
我們睡眠的錨鏈如此迅速排列整齊,
已然懸掛,從記憶中的繁星垂下細絲狀的末端。
一抹冰冷而不留痕跡的微笑……要怎樣的文字
才能扼殺這耳聾的月光?因為我們

已被超克。如今沒有哭喊,沒有利劍
得以牢繫或偏轉這潮汐節度的楔子,
月光慢條斯理的專橫,先是深愛
後又改變的月光……「世間

沒有這樣的東西,」你說,
心知我無法觸碰你的手也看不透
除了長眠的沙還在閃耀之外空無一物運轉

遠航

Where nothing turns but dead sands flashing.

"—And never to quite understand!" No,
In all the argosy of your bright hair I dreamed
Nothing so flagless as this piracy.

But now
Draw in your head, alone and too tall here.
Your eyes already in the slant of drifting foam;
Your breath sealed by the ghosts I do not know:
Draw in your head and sleep the long way home.

且罅隙間已不見眾神的天空。

「──永遠無法全然理解！」不，
在我夢中所有以你翠髮為名出航的大商船隊
從來沒有像這樣師出無名的海寇掠劫。

但現在
縮頸別再翹首，你孤伶伶在這裡頭探得太高。
你的眼睛已經因為飄沫而偏斜；
你的呼吸被我未識的鬼魂封印；
縮頸別再翹首，用沉睡度過回家的長路迢迢。

VI

Where icy and bright dungeons lift
Of swimmers their lost morning eyes,
And ocean rivers, churning, shift
Green borders under stranger skies,

Steadily as a shell secretes
Its beating leagues of monotone,
Or as many waters trough the sun's
Red kelson past the cape's wet stone;

O rivers mingling toward the sky
And harbor of the phoenix' breast—
My eyes pressed black against the prow,
—Thy derelict and blinded guest

Waiting, afire, what name, unspoke,
I cannot claim: let thy waves rear
More savage than the death of kings,
Some splintered garland for the seer.

VI

在冰冷而明亮的地牢升起之處
泳者他們的眼神在清晨迷離,
而海洋江河,翻攪起泡,在
陌生的天空下移動綠色的邊界,

如貝殼穩定分泌珍珠質
單調如一的脈動擊打一里又一里,
或如諸多水體流經海岬濡濕的石頭
飽餐太陽紅色的內龍骨;

哦朝向天空匯流於一的諸河
還有鳳凰胸口的港灣——
我的眼睛緊緊貼著船舷只見一片黑暗,
——您無主又冥瞽的船客

等待著,內心熾烈,什麼名字,欲言又止,
我卻不能有所主張:就讓您的波浪高升
比諸王之死更為蠻橫無道,
帶給先知某種碎裂的花環。

Beyond siroccos harvesting
The solstice thunders, crept away,
Like a cliff swinging or a sail
Flung into April's inmost day—

Creation's blithe and petalled word
To the lounged goddess when she rose
Conceding dialogue with eyes
That smile unsearchable repose—

Still fervid covenant, Belle Isle,
—Unfolded floating dais before
Which rainbows twine continual hair—
Belle Isle, white echo of the oar!

The imaged Word, it is, that holds
Hushed willows anchored in its glow.
It is the unbetrayable reply
Whose accent no farewell can know.

越過西洛可風帶來的收成
至點的雷鳴,躡手躡腳離開,
像一座懸崖搖蕩或像一張帆
激颺進四月最深處的白晝——

當慵懶斜倚的女神站起身來
造物主對她說的話語歡快好似口吐花瓣
眼神相交中退讓容許對話
眼中的笑意帶著無從探究的神祕安詳——

凝靜卻激切的盟約,美麗的島嶼,
——讓漂浮的講臺得見天日
讓彩虹在臺前編織綿延不絕的髮絲——
美麗的島嶼,船槳的白色回聲!

正是這以形象呈現的文字,其光輝
使歸於澄靜的柳樹下錨泊定其中。
這就是不會洩漏祕密的答覆
用這樣的口音告別無人知曉。

注釋

1 除第十五及第十六行外,本詩的每一行都是擷取自葛林柏格(Samuel Bernard Greenberg, 1893–1917)的詩作改寫而成。

2 威廉・索默(William Sommer, 1867–1949):美國現代主義畫家。索默出生於底特律,青年時期在平版印刷公司當學徒,自學成才,後前往慕尼黑學習美術;1907年後舉家定居克利夫蘭郊區。柯瑞恩十七歲時離家闖蕩,往返於紐約與克利夫蘭;廿二歲時與索默在克利夫蘭的書店結識,索默時年五十四,兩人結為忘年之交。這首詩描寫的就是索默的一幅靜物畫。

3 厄尼斯特・尼爾森(Ernest W. Nelson, 1879–1921):出生於挪威,十五歲赴美,就讀華盛頓的藝術學校。離開學校後被迫投入平版印刷業維生,在藝術與詩歌方面的發展因而中輟,後因經濟困頓而走上絕路。尼爾森曾與柯瑞恩通信,他建立了一所雅緻的私人圖書館,柯瑞恩也是訪客之一。

4 原詩的用字是「皮埃羅」(Pierrot),是法國默劇中的刻板角色,源自義大利藝術喜劇(commedia

dell'arte）。皮埃羅的固定扮相是一張塗白的臉，身著有褶邊領圈的寬大白色長襯衫和馬褲，往往帶著一絲孤獨而悲傷的氣息。

5　原詩的用字是「加岡圖亞」（Gargantua），拉伯雷（François Rabelais, *c.* 1483/1494–1553）《巨人傳》（*La vie de Gargantua et de Pantagruel, c.* 1532–*c.* 1564）中的第一代巨人君王。

6　亞述王拿步高（Nebuchadnezzar）的總司令，奉王命率大軍征討西方諸民族，唯獨猶太的以色列子民不肯屈服，封鎖山地隘口，據守山城拜突里雅（Bethulia）。敖羅斐乃率亞述大軍圍城三十四天，切斷水源，無水可喝的拜突里雅居民只願再忍五天。此時容貌姣美的寡婦友弟德（Judith）自願出城營救，她換下寡婦的苦衣換上錦衣，來到敖羅斐乃軍前，謊稱有情報來獻。敖羅斐乃迷戀友弟德的傾城國色，宴席間忘情暢飲，泥醉橫臥在床，於是友弟德取短劍趁機割下敖羅斐乃頭顱。亞述統帥身首異處，大軍潰散，拜突里雅居民大破亞述營盤。事見《舊約‧友弟德傳》。

7　洗者若翰（Baptist John）：按《瑪竇福音》與《馬爾谷福音》所載，黑落德（Herod Antipas, *c.* 20 BCE–*c.* 39 CE）娶嫂為妻，即兄弟斐理伯（Herod II, or Herod Philip I, *c.* 27 BCE–*c.* 34 CE）的妻子黑落狄雅（Herodias），因

而遭若翰譴責「你不可佔有你兄弟的妻子」。黑落德的生日宴會上，繼女（即莎樂美）獻舞大獲黑落德與賓客歡心，於是賞賜繼女，許以所求任何事物。未料懷恨在心的黑落狄雅慫恿女兒，要求將洗者若翰首級置於盤中呈上，黑落德無奈之下只得斬若翰於監。福音書中這段洗者若翰致命事蹟，也是王爾德（Oscar Wilde, 1854–1900))獨幕劇《莎樂美》（*Salomé*, 1896）的故事來源。

8　俄羅斯作曲家史特拉文斯基（Igor Stravinsky, 1882–1971）根據俄羅斯民間故事，創作了芭蕾舞劇《彼得魯什卡》（*Petrushka*, 1911）。故事的背景是1830年代的聖彼得堡，狂歡的廣場市集，一位老魔術師用笛聲喚醒了三只木偶：彼得魯什卡、芭蕾女伶與身著軍裝的摩爾人。柔弱的丑角彼得魯什卡心儀芭蕾女伶，他的示愛遭到鄙夷，心中頗不服氣摩爾人與女伶的情投意合。滿懷妒意的彼得魯什卡與情敵扭打，最後被盛怒的摩爾人用彎刀砍死。廣場觀賞木偶劇的群眾大驚失色，老魔術師舉起木偶安撫群眾；但鬆了口氣的群眾散去後，老魔術師卻看見彼得魯什卡的陰魂並未離開。

9　原文的用字是"Janus-faced"，亞努斯（Janus）是羅馬神話中掌管「大門／門道」的神祇。門有出入二途，一方面象徵入口與開端，另一方面象徵出口與終結，故神話中的亞努斯有兩副面孔，一回顧過去，一則展望未來。

亞努斯之名源自拉丁文的「門」（ianua），相傳羅馬士兵踏上征途，行伍必須先穿過亞努斯守護的拱門，這也是歐洲各國凱旋門的原型。亞努斯也是「開端」之神，故其名也成為西方語言中「一月」（January/Janvier/Januar/Gennaio）的來源。

10 和合本作「押沙龍」。達味王三子，以色列全境最俊美的男子，有一頭茂密長髮。其妹塔瑪爾（Tamar）遭同父異母的長兄阿默農（Amnon）誘姦，阿貝沙隆隱忍兩年，用計擊殺阿默農為妹復仇，後逃離耶路撒冷。多年後阿貝沙隆深獲以色列民心，心生造反之念，與父王達味的軍隊在厄弗辣因（Ephraim）森林遭遇。阿貝沙隆經過大橡樹下，長髮為樹枝所纏，坐騎離去，「身懸在天地間」。吊掛在樹上的阿貝沙隆無法掙脫，心中三箭後遭敵軍圍攻擊斃。事見《舊約‧撒慕爾紀下》第十三至第十八章。

11 亞述帝國都城，古美索不達米亞盛極一時的大城，後因亞述帝國滅亡（612 BCE）而衰落。公元 627 年，拜占庭皇帝希拉克略（Heraclius [Flavius Heraclius Augustus], c. 575–610–641）的軍隊攻入美索不達米亞，在尼尼微城遺址附近的平原擊潰波斯軍隊；這場戰役史稱「尼尼微之戰」，也終結了羅馬與波斯兩大帝國間持續六百多年的戰爭。歷代戰事中波斯奪走的黃金，在尼尼微之戰中又重回拜占庭軍隊之手，奪回的黃金總數計三百噸。

注釋　143

譯後記

我很喜歡「翻譯」這件事,無論視之為一份工作,抑或視之為一門研究領域。斷斷續續翻譯了幾年,譯作雖然不多,但每一本都是自己喜歡的書,也很享受每一本書的翻譯過程。這些過程對我來說一直都是充滿確定的:我很確定自己要怎麼翻譯原文(儘管仍有誤解原文的可能)。我猶清楚記得翻譯《大汗之國》(*The Chan's Great Continent: China in Western Minds*, 1998)[1] 和《現代的創痛》(*The Modern Agony as Shown in T. S. Eliot's Earlier Poems and Modern Chinese Poetry*, 1963)[2] 的時候,我曾經恭敬地把書中注腳提到的每一本書蒐集齊全,而且就是史景遷(Jonathan D[ermot] Spence, 1936–2021)和楊牧先生(1940–2020)使用的相同版本。這麼做的原因無他,就是為了確定:我必須確定自己完全理解作者的原意,有時候還可以發現原作的罅漏甚至差訛。我也相信翻譯是至為親密的閱讀行為(the most intimate act of reading),[3] 因此我首先必須做一位稱職的讀者,才能做一位合格的譯者。

接續結束《壞胚子》(*Rogues: True Stories of Grifters, Killers, Rebels and Crooks*, 2022)[4] 與《核戰倒數》(*One Minute to Midnight: Kennedy, Khrushchev, and Castro on the Brink of Nuclear*

War, 2008）[5] 二書的工作後，我隨即投入這本答應夏民兄已久的《白屋》翻譯。前兩本書一是出自近年暢銷非虛構類作家手筆的報導文學作品，一是重探六十年前古巴危機的外交與戰爭史偉構，就抽絲剝繭的情節進展著眼，兩本非虛構類作品雖未嘗不具備濃厚的文學性，然而兩本書的內容都出自確可信據的事實，建立在徵實的基礎上。其中雖頗不乏艱澀的用字與專有名詞，以致爬格子的進度迂緩，然而翻譯的過程始終充滿確定，也充滿閱讀的樂趣。不過這種一路相伴的確定，在我開始翻譯《白屋》之後，竟旋即如黃鶴杳然煙滅——我好像變得不知道怎麼翻譯了。

集子裡我首先選擇的是〈為浮士德與海倫成婚而作〉這首長詩，詎料沒開始幾行就敗下陣來。詩前取自瓊森（Ben Jonson, 1572-1637）《煉金術士》（*The Alchemist*, 1610）的題銘，與詩文間有什麼關係？多義的名詞在此做何解為佳？跨行的句子（enjambment）究竟該按原文斷句還是該依循通順的中文句法——又或者根本的問題是這究竟是跨行連續句抑或該分做兩行理解？句子裡有什麼我該理解卻錯過的隱喻嗎？這裡該加個注腳嗎？卜倫（Harold Bloom, 1930-2019）在《西方正典》（*The Western Canon: The Books and School of the Ages*, 1994）裡不只一次把克萊恩放在艾略特與史蒂文斯一脈相承自惠特曼的系譜中，謂其嚴謹於形式卻非空陳形似，而是在氣韻上得其神似，故稱其下筆成詩，「文采頗具艾略特與史蒂文斯之風，卻帶有惠特曼式的胸懷和態度」。[6] 懵懂之中對前半句大概有所體會，但要貫通卜倫的論點，勢必還得找出探討〈為浮士德與海倫成婚而作〉與《荒原》二作的論文研讀；至於後半則必然得再讀〈輪渡布魯克林〉（"Crossing Brooklyn Ferry," 1856）與《橋》（*The Bridge*, 1930）的緒言〈致布魯克林大橋〉（"To Brooklyn Bridge"）才能領略。儘管知道多聞闕疑的道理，但這麼一來一往開展閱讀地圖，就怕對讀詩非但沒有幫助，蹭蹬蹉跎之間恐怕那翻譯的確定感更不易復得。

嘗試譯完〈為浮士德與海倫成婚而作〉的第一節之後,我寄請夏民兄指點兩種譯法何者為佳,也藉此機會傾吐胸中鬱結的譯詩不確定感。夏民兄建議我其實只要按照自己對詩行的理解「譯」出來就好,不需要執著於自己這麼「讀」是不是正確,因為詩行的解釋本就不一定有標準答案,尤其是還需要經過翻譯。這讓我想起錢鍾書先生(1910–1998)在〈漢譯第一首英語詩〈人生頌〉及有關二三事〉裡引述的幾種論點:德哲赫爾德(Johann Gottfried Herder, 1744–1803)主張譯詩者乃「根據、依仿原詩而做出自己的詩」(Nachdichten, umdichten),如此一來,在原文與譯文的轉換之間,什麼是「詩」呢?佛洛斯特(Robert Frost, 1874–1963)以為詩就是

「在翻譯中喪失掉的東西」（What gets lost in translation）。錢先生對於譯詩顯然是悲觀的，因此繼而又援德國詩人摩根斯騰（Christian Morgenstern, 1871–1914）之言，謂詩歌翻譯「只分壞和次壞的兩種」（Es gibt nur schlechté Uebersetzungen und weniger schlechte），錢先生的結論是，「一個譯本以詩而論，也許不失為好『詩』，但做為原詩的複製，它終不免是壞『譯』」。[7]

法蘭柯（James Franco）自編自導自演的柯瑞恩傳記電影《斷塔》（*The Broken Tower*, 2011）以黑底白字的一段引文開場：「詩歌所以能激動人心，必然源於詩人使用的素材背後隱含的情感動能,故而詩人在用字遣詞上的擇取,並非著眼於字詞的邏輯(字面)意義,更多是因為聯想的含義。……語言構築塔樓與橋樑,本質卻必然是恆常流動不定(inevitably as fluid as always)。」[8] 這段話摘錄自柯瑞恩一篇自述寫詩目的與理論的短文,解釋他創作〈為浮士德與海倫成婚而作〉的理念:他意圖以現代措辭(字詞、象徵、隱喻),將古代人類的文化或神話體現為一個當代的近似版本,對他來說這其實就是在構建一座橋,「把所謂的古典經驗和我們當今喧騰擾嚷惶惑失序的世界中許多歧異的現實聯繫起來」。[9]

摸索之中經過這幾段文字的洗禮,我竟漸漸找回一種確定的感覺:知道詩的翻譯終究不可能完全表現詩人在原文中一氣呵成的巧思 —— 比方〈遠航〉第三節的 "Upon the steep floor flung from dawn to dawn / The silken skilled transmemberment of song" 兩行,那連續節奏中的頭韻、不完全韻(slant rhyme)和自創新字 —— 如雪萊(Percy Bysshe Shelley, 1792–1822)在〈為詩辯護〉("A Defence of Poetry," 1821, 1840)中論聲音與思想間的關係,認為譯詩乃勞而無功之舉,蓋詩人之語言中,其聲音往往以某種始終如一而和諧的形式重現(recurrence of sound),失之則不成其為詩。[10] 知道詩文的意義恆常流動不定,知道集子裡像〈擁有〉

這樣的詩不可能從技術層面解釋[11]，知道詩人有權從書籍或身邊任何實用資源中汲取靈感[12]，而我終究不能像翻譯前面幾本書那樣追求徵實考證的確定。知道自己因此只需跟隨自己的理解與感動，忠實翻譯下去。

於是懷抱著虔敬，懷抱著這樣的確定，我譯完《白屋》。

長樂林熙強
甲辰年林鍾之月
Strong and content I travel the open road.

1　史景遷著，林熙強譯：《大汗之國：西方眼中的中國》（*The Chan's Great Continent: China in Western Minds*, 1998），二十週年紀念版。新北：臺灣商務印書館，2018。

2　楊牧著，林熙強譯：《現代的創痛：艾略特早期詩作與現代中文詩》（*The Modern Agony as Shown in T. S. Eliot's Earlier Poems and Modern Chinese Poetry*, 1963）。收入楊牧全集編輯委員會編：《楊牧全集》24【別卷 II：集外集（二）：文論】，頁 91–230。臺北：洪範書店有限公司，2024。

3　語本史碧娃克（Gayatri Chakravorty Spivak, 1942– ）於 "The Politics of Translation" 中所言，見 *Destabilizing Theory: Contemporary Feminist Debates*, edited by Michèle Barrett and Anne Phillips (Stanford: Stanford University Press, 1992), pp. 178 & 181。

4　派崔克・拉登・基夫（Patrick Radden Keefe）著，林熙強、吳侑達、汪冠岐、王婉茜譯：《壞胚子：騙子、殺手、叛徒與無賴的真實故事》（*Rogues: True Stories of Grifters, Killers, Rebels and Crooks*, 2022）。臺北：黑體文化，2024。

5 麥可‧達博思（Michael Dobbs）著，林熙強譯：《核戰倒數》（*One Minute to Midnight: Kennedy, Khrushchev, and Castro on the Brink of Nuclear War*, 2008）。臺北：凌宇出版，2023。

6 見 Harold Bloom, *The Western Canon: The Books and School of the Ages* (New York: Harcourt Brace, 1994), pp. 33, 265, 476 等處。

7 見錢鍾書：〈漢譯第一首英語詩〈人生頌〉及有關二三事〉（"Longfellow's 'A Psalm of Life'—the First English Poem Translated into Chinese—and Several Other Related Matters," 1948），在氏著：《七綴集》（北京：生活‧讀書‧新知三聯書店，2002），頁 143–144。

8 See Hart Crane, "General Aims and Theories" (1937), in *The Complete Poems and Selected Letters and Prose of Hart Crane*, edited with an Introduction and notes by Brom Weber (Garden City, NY: Anchor Books/Doubleday, 1966), pp. 221 & 223.

9 Ibid., p. 217.

10 See Percy Bysshe Shelley, "A Defence of Poetry," in *The Complete Works of Percy Bysshe Shelley*, Volume VII: Prose, edited by Roger Ingpen and Walter E[dwin] Peck (London: Ernest Benn; New York: Gordian Press, 1965), p. 114.

11 Crane, "General Aims and Theories," p. 222.

12 Ibid., p. 218.

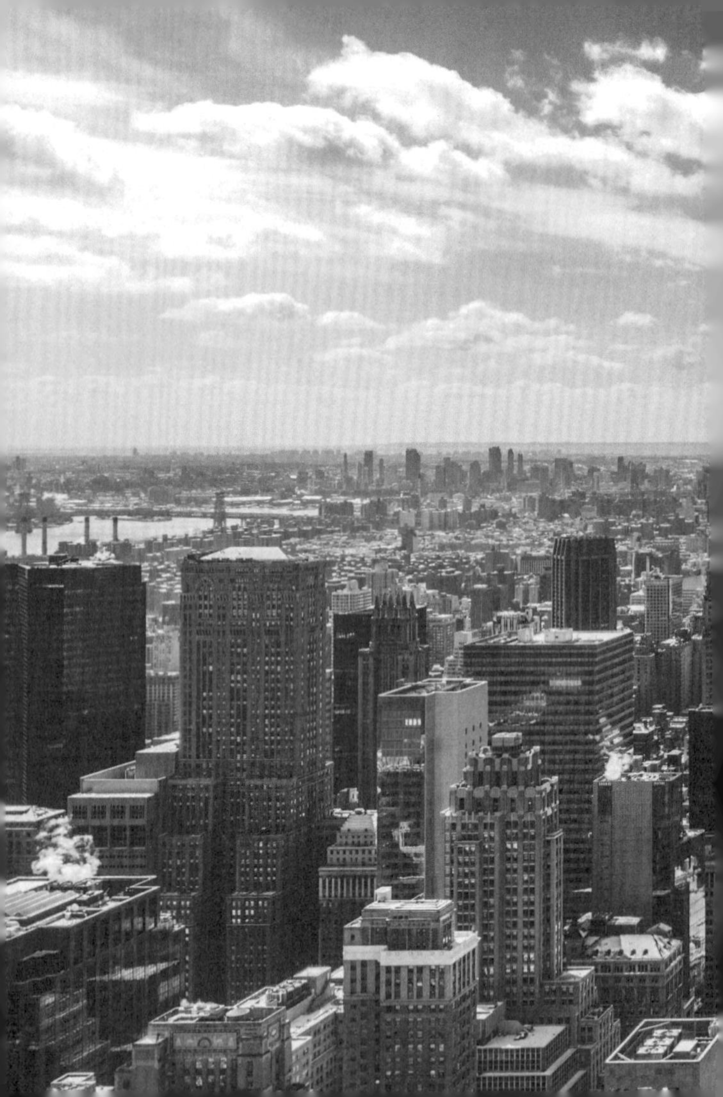

言寺 98

白屋

作　　者	Hart Crane 哈特・柯瑞恩
譯　　者	林熙強
總 編 輯	陳夏民
責任編輯	郭正偉
譯文校對	王建文
書籍設計	陳昭淵

出　　版	comma books
	地址｜桃園市 330 中央街 11 巷 4-1 號
	網站｜www.commabooks.com.tw
	電話｜03-335-9366
總 經 銷	知己圖書股份有限公司
地　　址	台北公司｜台北市 106 大安區辛亥路一段 30 號 9 樓
	電話｜02-2367-2044
	傳真｜02-2363-5741
	台中公司｜台中市 407 工業區 30 路 1 號
	電話｜04-2359-5819
	傳真｜04-2359-5493

製　　版	軒承彩色印刷製版有限公司
印　　刷	通南彩色印刷有限公司
裝　　訂	智盛裝訂股份有限公司
倉　　儲	書林出版有限公司
電子書總經銷	聯合線上股份有限公司

初版一刷　2025 年 7 月
ＩＳＢＮ　978-626-7606-11-7
定　　價　新台幣 350 元

版權所有・翻印必究 Printed in Taiwan

國家圖書館出版品預行編目 (CIP) 資料

白屋 / 哈特．柯瑞恩著；林熙強譯 初版 _ 桃園市：逗點文創結社
2025.5_160 面 _10.5× 14.5cm（言寺 98）｜譯自：White Buildings
ISBN 978-626-7606-11-7(平裝)｜874.51｜113020670

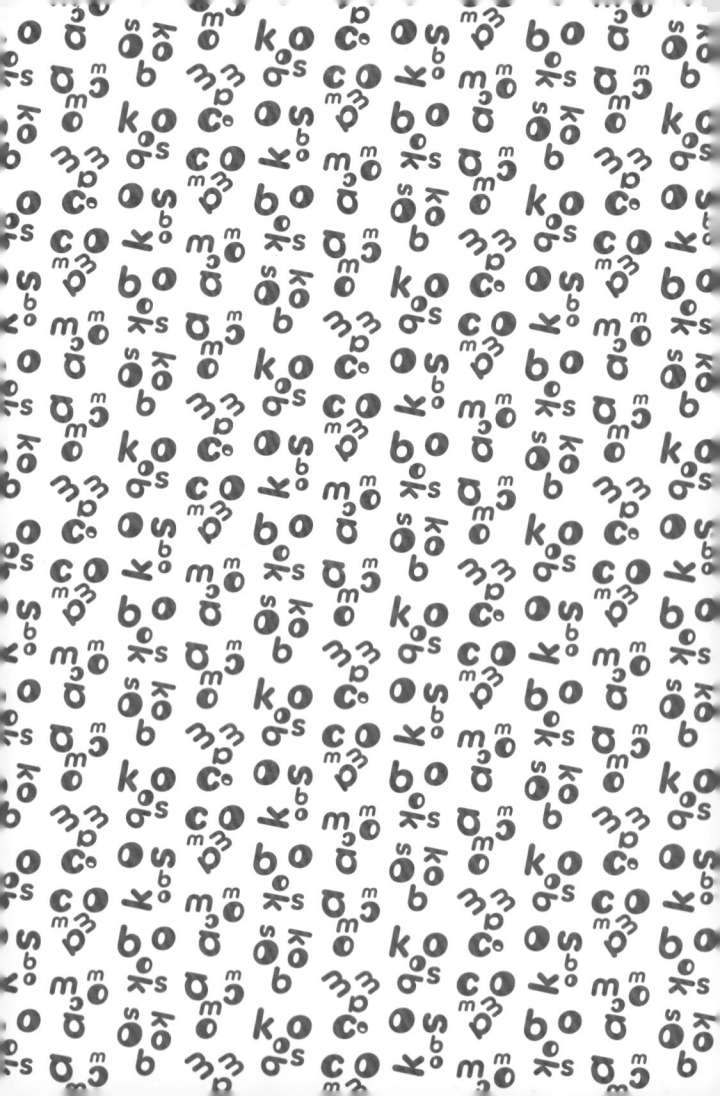